active minds®

Rhyming Words

cat

hat

dog

frog

king

ring

doll

ball

plane

train

tree

ski

bug

mug

pail

snail

bear

pear

fox

box

moon

spoon

car

star

cake

shake

tie

pie

mouse

house

hen

pen

pig

wig

goat

boat

duck

truck

fish

dish

Photography © Shutterstock, Photo Disc,
Siede Preis Photography, and Brian Warling Photography

Published by Sequoia Kids Media,
an imprint of Sequoia Publishing & Media, LLC

Sequoia Publishing & Media, LLC.,
a division of Phoenix International Publications, Inc.

8501 West Higgins Road, Chicago, Illinois 60631

Paperback edition published in 2022 by Crabtree Publishing Company
ISBN 978-1-6499-6655-1 Printed in China

Customer Service: orders@crabtreebooks.com

Crabtree Classroom
A division of Crabtree Publishing Company
347 Fifth Avenue, Suite 1402-145
New York, NY, 10016

Crabtree Classroom
A division of Crabtree Publishing Company
616 Welland Ave.
St. Catharines, ON, L2M 5V6